SHIMMER and Shine ™

Show Your LOVE!

Adapted by Mary Tillworth from the script "Happy Wishaversary" by Dustin Ferrer

Illustrated by Dave Aikins

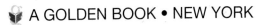 A GOLDEN BOOK • NEW YORK

© 2016 Viacom International Inc. All rights reserved. Published in the United States by Golden Books, an imprint of Random House Children's Books, a division of Penguin Random House LLC, 1745 Broadway, New York, NY 10019, and in Canada by Penguin Random House Canada Limited, Toronto. Golden Books, A Golden Book, A Big Golden Book, the G colophon, and the distinctive gold spine are registered trademarks of Penguin Random House LLC. Nickelodeon, Shimmer and Shine, and all related titles, logos, and characters are trademarks of Viacom International Inc.
T#: 502469
randomhousekids.com
ISBN 978-1-5247-1603-5
Printed in the United States of America
10 9 8 7 6 5 4 3 2 1

One morning, Shimmer and Shine leapt out of bed and flew from their rooms. They could barely contain their excitement. It was their wishaversary, a special day to celebrate their friendship with Leah!

In the kitchen, the two genies began to make their wishaversary gift for Leah. Into a golden bowl they put two dragon eggs, a pinch of stardust, a dash of moonlight, and some sparkles.

Shimmer meant to add only a few sparkles, but she accidentally added the whole bottle!

"You can never have too many sparkles!" she giggled. "All we need now are our special gems!"

The twins chanted, *"Mix these gems and sparkles together to make our friend the best gift ever!"*

Poof! There was a puff of magical smoke, and a small box rose out of the golden bowl.

Shimmer gasped. "It's perfect!" she said as a red ribbon wrapped itself around the box.

"Leah is going to love it," agreed Shine.

Shimmer and Shine jumped onto their magic carpet.
Tala and Nahal hopped up, too. They soared above pink
and blue palaces, over a rainbow, and down through the
glistening clouds, leaving Zahramay Falls far behind.

Moments later, the genies flew out of Leah's bottle necklace. "Happy wishaversary!" they cheered.

Shine handed Leah the sparkling present.

"We made you a special gift," she said.

Leah untied the bow and opened her gift.

"A bracelet! Thank you!" She slipped it over her wrist—and began to float!

"Whenever the bracelet is on your wrist, you can fly like a genie!" Shimmer explained.

Just then, a puppy barked outside the window. It was Zac's dog, Rocket.

Leah gasped. "It's Zac! Hide before he sees you!" she told the genies.

Shimmer and Shine dove under the table. As Zac opened the door, they grabbed Leah's ankles so she wouldn't drift away.

Zac came in with a new video game—*Disco Dragons Dance Party II*! He headed into the living room. "I'm not leaving until we beat this game!"

"How do I get down from here?" Leah asked the genies.

Shimmer snapped her fingers. "It's our wishaversary! And what better way to celebrate than by making a wish?"

"Good idea!" Leah closed her eyes. "For my first wish, I wish I could stop floating."

Shimmer spun her bracelets. *"Boom, Zahramay! First wish of the day!"*

"Shimmer and Shine, stop floating divine!" chanted Shine.

The bracelet fell from Leah's wrist—and snapped itself onto Rocket's leg! Leah was back down on the ground, but now Zac's puppy was heading toward the ceiling!

"Oh, no!" Leah tried to jump and grab Rocket—and missed. "He's going into the living room. We can't let Zac see Rocket flying!"

As Rocket sailed through the living room, Leah distracted Zac with snacks while Shimmer and Shine tried to catch the flying puppy.

"Huh. Onions, lemons, and some mustard?" Zac shrugged. "I was thinking more chips or popcorn, but I guess this works."

"I'll be *riiiight* back," Leah promised as Rocket drifted into the hallway.

In the hallway, Leah saw Rocket flapping his ears and zipping around!

"When I made your bracelet fall off, I didn't mean to make Rocket fly," Shimmer said. "I really made a mistake with this one."

"That's okay, Shimmer. You didn't know the bracelet would land on Rocket." Leah smiled. "Plus, a flying dog is pretty cool."

Shine conjured up a butterfly net. "This will help us catch Rocket!" She tried to snag the flying pup, but he was too fast!

Leah had an idea. "For my second wish, I wish Rocket would land."

"Boom, Zahramay! Second wish of the day!" Shimmer said, spinning her bracelets. *"Shimmer and Shine, Rocket land divine!"*

A cloud of magic sparkles filled the air. When it cleared, a silver and pink rocket stood in the hallway!

Leah scratched her head. "I was hoping that Rocket the dog would land on the floor, not a rocket ship."

She and the genies tried to push the rocket out of the hallway—but it wouldn't budge!

"I wish this rocket would move!" sighed Leah.

Leah hadn't meant to use her last wish . . . but it was too late. Shimmer clapped her hands. *"Boom, Zahramay! Third wish of the day! Shimmer and Shine, move the rocket divine!"*

The rocket rumbled to life and zoomed around the corner, crashing into everything in sight!

Zac came into the hallway. "Leah, you can start playing the game. I'll meet you back in the living room," he called as he headed into the bathroom.

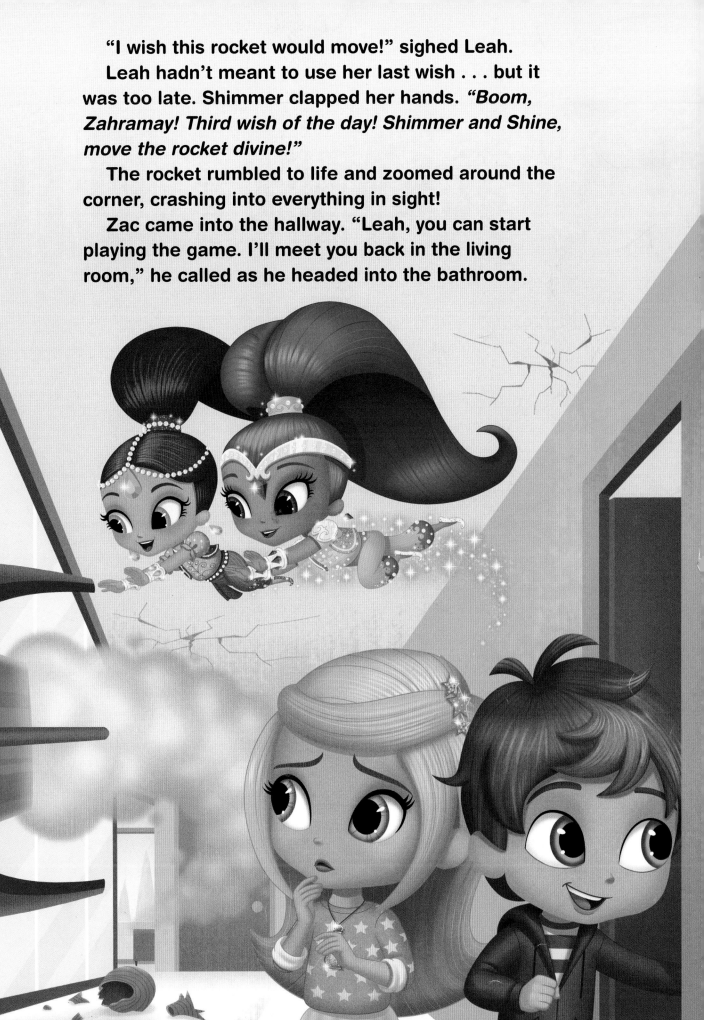

Leah ran into the living room. The rocket was smashing everything! Shine waved her puppy-catching net. She snagged the top of the rocket. "I gotcha!" she cried. But the rocket was so powerful, it whisked her out of the house!

"Uh, Shimmer, a little help?" called Shine.
The two genies wrestled the rocket back to the ground.
"Whew. At least one rocket isn't flying," sighed Shine.
"Thanks, guys!" Leah turned toward the house. "Now I've gotta get back before Zac's done."

"Whoa! You really made a mess playing the game!" Zac said when he returned. He stared at the rocket wreckage. There were flipped chairs, strewn snacks, and cracked walls!

Leah coughed. "Things got kinda out of control."

Zac shrugged. "I get super excited when I play video games, too!" He grabbed a controller and began to play alongside Leah.

Leah quietly snuck the controller to Tala and crept out to help the genies.

Leah found Shimmer and Shine in the messy hallway. "Now we have to figure out a way to clean up the house *and* get my bracelet back from Rocket without any wishes."

"Sorry, Leah," said Shimmer. "I didn't mean to make a mistake."

"From now on, no more flying rockets," promised Shine.

"Wait," said Shimmer. "If flying made this mess, then flying can help clean it up!"

The genies flew around, tidying up the hallway. They hung the pictures back on the walls, straightened out the books, and put everything back in place. When they were done, the house looked as good as new!

"Seeing all that flying gives me an idea. Think you can float Rocket's dog treats over here?" asked Leah.

Shimmer got the dog treats and used one to lure Rocket down to the ground. Leah slipped the bracelet off his leg.

"The Rocket has landed!" cheered Shine.

And it was just in time, too. Zac had finished the video game and was ready to go home.

After Zac left, the genies met Leah in the backyard.

"Now that Zac's gone, do you want to try flying again?" asked Shimmer.

"Sure! If you guys do it with me." Leah slipped on the bracelet. "I'm flying! I'm really flying! Woo-hoo!"

"Great job!" Shimmer told her.

"Hey! I still haven't given you guys your present." Leah zoomed into the house and returned with a gift-wrapped box. She handed it to the two genies.

The genies unwrapped their gift.
"It's a scrapbook for pictures of all our
adventures together," explained Leah.
"Thank you, Leah," said Shimmer.
"It's perfect!" laughed Shine.

They had opened their presents, but there was still one more surprise. Shine waved her hand, and the rocket ship soared into the night sky and burst into a shower of beautiful fireworks!

"This has been the best wishaversary ever," said Shimmer.

"We fixed our mistakes, and the day turned out great!" Leah hugged her two genies. "Happy wishaversary, Shimmer and Shine."